This Little Tiger book belongs to:

For Connie and Christien,
Thomas and Dominic
and Mrs Murphy

~ R T

LITTLE TIGER PRESS
1 The Coda Centre, 189 Munster Road, London SW6 6AW
First published in Great Britain 2001
This edition published 2001
Text and illustrations copyright © Rory Tyger 2001
Rory Tyger has asserted his right to be identified as the
author and illustrator of this work under the Copyright,
Designs and Patents Act, 1988
A CIP catalogue record for this book is available
from the British Library
All rights reserved • ISBN 978-1-85430-721-7
Printed in China
4 6 8 10 9 7 5

newton

Rory Tyger

LITTLE TIGER PRESS
London

CREAK, CREAK, CRE-E-EAK

Newton woke up suddenly. There was a funny noise somewhere in the room.

"Don't be frightened," he told Woffle. "There's always an explanation for everything."

He gave each of his toys a special cuddle so they wouldn't be scared.

CREAK, CREAK, CRE-E-EAK
went the noise again.

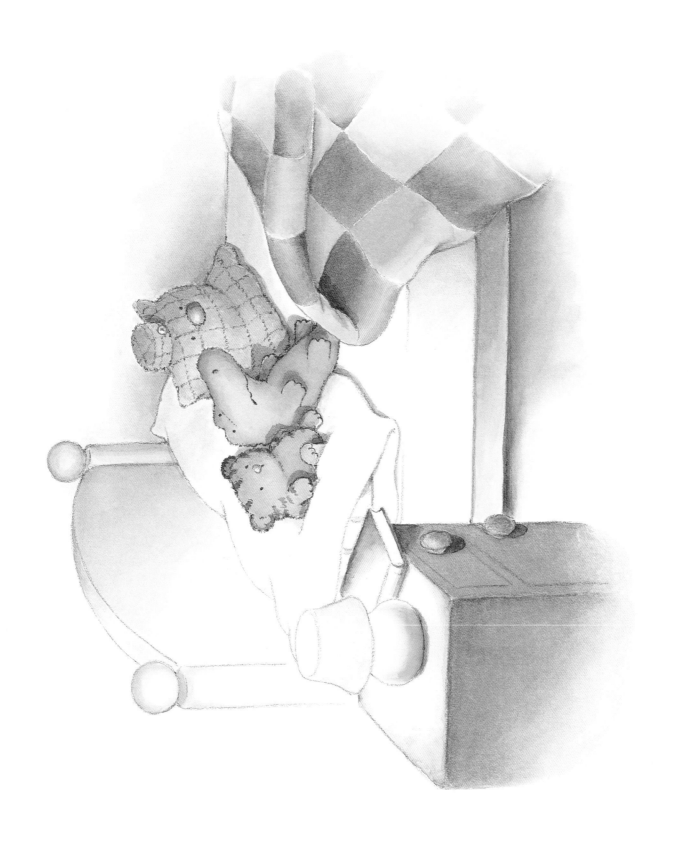

Newton got out of bed and turned on the light.
He walked across the room . . . .

"See, toys," he said. "There's nothing to be frightened of. It's only the wardrobe door!"

Newton went back to bed again.

FLAP! FLAP! FLAP!
What was that? Was it a ghost?

Once more Newton got out of bed. He wasn't really scared, but he took his bravest toy, Snappy, just in case. He tiptoed, very quietly, towards the noise.

FLAP! FLAP! FLAP!

"Of course!" said Newton . . .

"You were very brave,
Snappy," he said, as
he closed the window.

"Just what I thought."
It was his bedroom curtains,
flapping in the breeze.
"I'll soon sort those out,"
said Newton.

SPLISH!

SPLASH!

SPLISH!

Another noise!

Newton looked outside. It wasn't raining.
Besides, the noise wasn't coming from outside.

Nor was it coming from his bedroom. What was it?

"Stay right there, you two," said Newton, "while I look around."

He wasn't the tiniest bit afraid. He was just taking Snappy with him for company.

Newton crept down the corridor. It was very spooky, especially in the dark corners.

SPLISH! SPLASH! SPLOSH!
went the noise.

Very, very quietly, Newton opened the bathroom door . . .

"Of course, we knew it was the bathroom tap, didn't we, Snappy," said Newton.

Newton turned off the tap, and tiptoed back down the corridor. "Shh," he said to Snappy, just in case *something* in the dark corners sprang out at them.

"You can go to sleep now," he told all his toys.

Before he got into bed, Newton pulled back the curtains – just to check. It was very, very quiet outside. "No more funny noises," said Newton.

RUMBLE! RUMBLE! RUMBLE!

"Oh no!" cried Newton. "What's that?"

Newton listened very hard. Not a sound. He was just beginning to think he hadn't heard anything at all when . . . .

RUMBLE! RUMBLE! RUMBLE!

There it was again!

Newton peered under his bed.
Nothing there at all – except for an
old sweet he'd forgotten about.
    "Don't worry," said Newton. "We'll
soon find out what it is."

RUMBLE!
Newton listened
very hard.

RUMBLE!
Newton stood
very still.

RUMBLE! went the noise.
And suddenly Newton knew
exactly what it was!

Newton padded downstairs, and into the kitchen. He helped himself to a large glass of milk and two thick slices of bread and honey. And now he could hear no

RUMBLE! RUMBLE! RUMBLE!

at all, because . . .

. . . the rumbling had been his empty tummy!

Newton went upstairs again, and told his toys about his rumbling tummy.

"There's always an explanation for everything," said Newton, as he climbed back into bed.

"Goodnight, everyone . . ."

. . . Sleep tight!"

SNORE, SNORE, SNORE,

went Newton.